Magic Pony

The Champion Jumper

"It's show jumping," said Annie. "We can watch it together."

"Not watch it," said the pony. "Do it! I've got it all worked out."

Annie stepped back in surprise. "You mean, me and you do the show-jumping competition?"

"That's exactly what I mean. You don't think we've done all that nighttime show-jumping practice for nothing, do you?"

**Join Annie on all her adventures
with Ned, the Magic Pony!**

Magic Pony
The Champion Jumper

Elizabeth Lindsay

Illustrated by John Eastwood

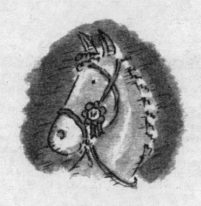

A
LITTLE APPLE
PAPERBACK

SCHOLASTIC INC.
New York Toronto London Auckland Sydney
Mexico City New Delhi Hong Kong Buenos Aires

For Emma

No part of this publication may be reproduced in whole or in part, or stored in a retrieval system, or transmitted in any form or by any means, electronic, mechanical, photocopying, recording, or otherwise, without written permission of the publisher. For information regarding permission, write to Scholastic Children's Books, Commonwealth House, 1-19 New Oxford Street, London WC1A 1NU, UK.

ISBN 0-439-44653-8
Text copyright © 1998 Elizabeth Lindsay.
Illustrations copyright © 1998 John Eastwood.

All rights reserved. Published by Scholastic Inc., 557 Broadway, New York, NY 10012, by arrangement with Scholastic Children's Books, Scholastic Ltd. SCHOLASTIC, Little Apple, and associated logos are trademarks and/or registered trademarks of Scholastic Inc.

12 11 10 9 8 7 6 5 4   12 13 14 15 /0

Printed in the U.S.A.
First Scholastic printing, March 2003

Chapter 1

Be My Groom!

Annie awoke with a shiver of excitement and sat up. At the end of the bed Tabitha uncurled when the feet she'd been lying on were suddenly gone.

"I'm going to be a groom today," Annie cried, tossing back the comforter. It covered Tabitha like a cloud and, being a cat who liked to be cozy, she curled up again underneath. Annie looked at her clock. Ten to six. The alarm would ring in ten minutes. Already wide awake, she pressed the off button and jumped out of bed. Next, she pulled back the curtains and let in the sunshine, turning quickly to the pony poster on the wall above her chest of drawers. She expected to see a handsome chestnut pony stare her straight in the eye but, to her surprise, the picture was empty.

"The magic's working," she cried. "Ned's come out of his poster. I must find him before I go."

She dropped to her hands and knees and looked under the bed.

"Ned, I'm going to a horse show with Penelope Potter and Pebbles. Penelope asked me to be her groom." Annie hoped to find a tiny chestnut pony there. Instead she found herself talking to the gloom and the dust balls. She wondered where else to look. "Why does everything exciting have to happen on the same day?"

When the pony in the poster did come alive, the world became a place of possibilities where anything could happen! Most often, Ned was a glossy picture on the wall but, with the magic, he became a real, warm, huggable pony. Sometimes he was the same size as Pebbles and sometimes as tiny as Percy, the smallest of the three china ponies on her bedroom windowsill. Most important, Ned was her biggest secret.

She turned to look under the chest of drawers, just in case, but he wasn't there, either. A quick glance at the windowsill showed Esmerelda, Prince, and Percy standing alone in the dazzling sunlight. If only Ned would stop hiding and become his big self, she could fling her arms around his neck and give him a hug.

Annie sat back on her haunches, remembering what Jamie had said the night before. "You must be crazy to go as Penelope's groom. You'll have to take orders and do what she tells you all day." His words were said to be helpful, Annie knew, and, from an older brother who often ignored her, it was nice. But Jamie didn't understand that taking orders was worth it if it meant she could go to the horse show.

At least that was what Annie had felt yesterday. She had thought only of grooming Pebbles and watching the show jumping. But today, now that Ned's magic was working, she could actually be riding, too. Not at a horse show, maybe, but there was the log to jump in Winchway Wood and lots of places to gallop. She sighed, then, noticing her bedroom door was open just enough for a tiny pony to squeeze through, realized that Ned had already gone.

No one else was awake yet, although Mom had promised to get up at six to make Annie's sandwiches and see her off. She looked at the clock — she had five minutes to find him — and tiptoed onto the landing. Mom and Dad's bedroom door was shut and so was Jamie's. She peeked into the bathroom, hoping to see Ned canter across the bath mat, but the bathroom was empty.

Downstairs, the door between the living room and dining room was closed, but moving on she found the door to the kitchen wide open. The *bang-bang* of the cat flap startled her. It took her a moment or two to realize that the banging wasn't Tabitha. Tabitha was upstairs under the covers. She hurried through the dining room to the kitchen. There was not a hint of a tiny pony anywhere, so she scurried back to open the curtains in the living room and looked outside. The yard was empty. If only Ned would change to his big self so she could see him! A miniature pony could be galloping anywhere.

Annie tapped impatient fingers against the windowpane. She longed for someone to help her search, but if you have a secret, then you can't tell. There was just one person Annie suspected might know of Ned's magic and that was Mr. Cosby at

Cosby's Magic Emporium. When he had taken Ned's poster from the window display on the day she bought it, she was sure Mr. Cosby had winked at her. But Mr. Cosby was in town, miles away, so that was no help. Time ticked by and Annie knew she had to hurry or be late. After all, she was going to be a groom at the horse show. She had promised Penelope, hadn't she?

From upstairs came the *beep-beep-beep* of Mom's alarm clock. She'd better be quick. If she kept Penelope waiting, there would be trouble. Even so, it was terrible to think of missing Ned's magic. She raced for the bathroom, jumping two stairs at a time, and bumped into Mom on the landing.

"Steady, Annie. I was just coming to wake you."

"Already awake," said Annie. "Can I go first in the bathroom?"

"Be quick," said Mom. "I'll go down and make your sandwiches. What kind would you like?"

"Anything." Annie was already closing the bathroom door.

By the time she had brushed her teeth and washed, Annie knew she had to keep her promise. She had to go to the horse show. Ned's magic would work again. She could wait until next time. She flung her towel at the rack and raced across the landing. Penelope was expecting her at the stable yard at six-fifteen. She was nearly late.

Back in her bedroom, she quickly pulled on her jeans and sneakers, grabbed a clean T-shirt, and struggled into her sweatshirt. She was ready.

"Good-bye," she said, giving a quick pat to Percy's sun-warmed back. He was facing the window, the way she had left him. "Wish me luck, you three. I've never been a groom before."

Across the lane in Pebbles's field, a chestnut pony cantered toward one of Penelope's practice jumps.

"Ned," Annie gasped. With a leap and a bound, the pony soared over the jump, his mane flying, no longer the tiny pony he must have been to have gone out through the cat flap. Now he was as big and as handsome as Pebbles. Spellbound, she watched him turn for a row of blue plastic barrels. The jump was magnificent.

Why hadn't he woken her up? Why had he gone off by himself? She hadn't even been able to tell him she was going to the horse show with Penelope. But even more serious, if he didn't watch out, Penelope would see him. Any minute now, she would arrive in her stable yard.

Annie, wanting more than anything to run outside and jump on Ned's back, wished they could gallop away for a day in Winchway Wood. She took a deep breath. Why not?

She raced from her bedroom and pounded down the stairs. She was at the front door in a flash. Wrenching it open, she ran down the path and was through the gate like a whirlwind. She swung herself to the top of the field gate and was about to jump onto the grass when she saw the chestnut pony had gone. An uncomfortable feeling welled up inside her. Was Ned avoiding her? Didn't he want to be her friend anymore?

Mom called from the front door. "Annie, what are you doing? Come and get your backpack. You're going to be late."

Annie dropped from the gate. If Ned didn't want her to find him, she knew she wouldn't. She tried not to feel hurt. She would leave her bedroom window open so that he could take the easy way back to his poster by jumping up the fig-tree leaves to her windowsill. She would just have to hurry up and go. There was no other choice. Outside the stable yard gate, Penelope beckoned to her.

"Get a move on, Annie. It's six-twenty. You're supposed to give Pebbles his breakfast." Jamie was right. The day was going to be filled with a stream of orders. Oh, well, she supposed that was better than knowing Ned's magic was working and not being able to find him.

Chapter 2

To the Horse Show

Annie hurried into the house to get her backpack from the hook in the closet under the stairs. In the kitchen, Mom was putting the finishing touches on her picnic.

"I've made plenty," she said when Annie arrived. "Hold out your hand." Annie did so and Mom put two dollars in her palm. "Pocket money and some for an ice cream."

"Do they have ice cream at horse shows?"

"I don't know," said Mom. "But they might."

Annie crammed her sandwich box, a can of lemonade, and a bottle of water into her backpack.

"Here," said Mom, "and these." She added two apples and a banana. "That should keep you going."

"Thanks, Mom. There's something I've got to do upstairs. Hang on to this!" Annie thrust her backpack into Mom's hands and raced for the stairs. She burst into her bedroom, causing a startled cat to peep out from under the comforter.

"It's only me, Tabs." Annie pulled open the top drawer of her chest of drawers. "I need my coin purse." Unzipping it, she added the two dollars to the money already there before stuffing it in her pocket. Then she opened the window just enough for a tiny pony to come in and raced back downstairs to the hall.

Mom handed Annie the backpack, planted a kiss on her forehead, and pulled the front door open. "Have a nice time."

Annie ran down the path, gave Mom a wave, and, with a last look over the gate, hurried down the path to the stable yard.

By the time she arrived, Pebbles had already eaten his breakfast. He was tied up outside his stable and Penelope was undoing his tail, which had spent the night cocooned in a blue bandage to keep it clean.

"Where've you been, Annie? You should have been here ages ago. You can start with the mucking out." Annie dumped her backpack on the tack room floor.

"Can I help with the grooming?"

"You can when you've finished." With a sigh, Annie got the wheelbarrow. "And fill a hay net to take in the trailer."

While Annie was busy with her

pitchfork, Mrs. Potter backed across the road and into the yard, turning the car to stop in front of the horse trailer, ready for hitching up.

"Hello, Annie," she said when Annie wheeled the barrow past on her way to the manure pile. "Good of you to help."

By the time the stable was neat and clean and Mrs. Potter had tied the hay net inside the trailer, Penelope was looking mighty flustered.

"Wash and dry Pebbles's hooves, Annie. Then I can put on the hoof oil," she said.

Annie sighed and picked up a bucket. "Can I do the oiling?"

"OK," said Penelope unexpectedly. "I'll put the tack in the car." And she handed over the can and the brush. "You can body brush him, too, if you like. He could do with a little more gloss. Then put on his traveling rug." Penelope set off for the tack room. "I'll do his tail bandage and boots." Annie grinned. At last she had something interesting to do.

"Haven't you got his rug on yet?" said Penelope, returning a few minutes later, arms full of pony traveling boots. Annie hurried to obey. Penelope dumped

the boots and pulled out a tail bandage from the waistband of her jodhpurs. She bandaged Pebbles's tail with the quick, deft movements of someone who had done it many times before.

"If you keep on being my groom, you can do all this," she said. "Then I'll be able to relax and get myself ready for the jumping. Real show jumpers always have grooms. Then they can concentrate on what's important."

Tail bandage in place, Penelope started hooking the Velcro on the traveling boots that Annie knew were necessary in case Pebbles knocked his legs in the trailer. By the time they had finished, Pebbles looked extremely handsome and was ready to be loaded into the trailer.

Up until this moment, Annie hadn't thought about how horrible it was going to be leaving Ned behind.

"Put the grooming box in the back of the car," said Penelope.

"Stand back, Annie," said Mrs. Potter, giving a different order. "It can go in when I've backed around." Annie stepped out of the way while the trailer was reversed into position. She felt a thrill of excitement when Pebbles was led in and the ramp was raised. They were ready to go.

"Don't waste time," Penelope snapped. "Let's go."

Annie hurried to the back of the car and, pulling open the door, found all kinds of things scattered around. Penelope's riding clothes for one thing. She pushed aside a bag of colored bandages and slid in the grooming box. The moment she slammed the door, the engine started.

"Get in," shouted Penelope from the front window. Annie climbed aboard. As soon as her bottom was in place, they were off.

"Make sure you don't get Pebbles's hair everywhere, Annie. It's such a nuisance to get off the seats," said Mrs. Potter. Annie fastened her seat belt and, as they drove into the road, obligingly brushed at her legs. "Penelope, you're going to have to read the directions for me."

"Me? Why can't Annie do it?"

"Because you're sitting in the front. It's easier for me to hear."

Penelope sat in a silent smolder; Annie slumped in the backseat. This was going to be a day to remember, all right. Glancing out of the window, she was surprised to see Ned trot across the stable yard. Then he was lost to her view. She took a quick look to see if Mrs. Potter and Penelope had seen him. No, Mrs. Potter was concentrating on her driving and Penelope was struggling with the road map.

Annie stretched around to glimpse a flash of chestnut in the road. Was Ned going to follow them? Common sense

told her it was impossible. A loose pony galloping after a horse trailer would soon attract attention. Her best hope was that, by the time she came home again, Ned would be safely back in his picture.

They breezed along the open road, following Penelope's directions. "Oh, no!" said Annie and suddenly sat up. "I've left my backpack in the tack room!"

"Tough," said Penelope. "It's too late to go back for it now. You'll just have to manage without it."

Annie's tummy rumbled just to remind her of where breakfast was, and she realized Jamie was right. She must be crazy. She'd missed Ned in order to be bossed around all day by Penelope, and now she was going to go hungry, too. She curled up in her seat trying to cheer herself up with a horse-show daydream. But the only picture she could imagine was of Ned, left behind in the road, watching them go.

Chapter 3

Going It Alone

It didn't take as long as Annie thought it would to drive to the show ground. They came to a white sign that read HORSE SHOW, with an arrow directing them down a narrow lane. Annie sat up, not wanting to miss a thing. The show ground was a large field. It was marked out by the tops of parked trucks and the pale top of a tent visible above the hedge.

They drove in through the gate to find an amazing number of trucks and horse trailers parked in several long rows. There were ponies everywhere — bays, blacks, grays, roans, some tied to their vehicles, some being groomed, some ridden. There were more ponies and riders in one place than Annie could count and the most exciting bustle of preparation she had ever seen.

Annie didn't want to miss a thing and clung on, her eyes bright, as they bumped across the grass. Between the trucks and trailers, she saw the bright colors of the jumps standing ready in the show-jumping ring. *If only, if only it could be me*, she thought.

At last, Mrs. Potter found a place beside a big blue horse trailer.

"We're next to Anneli Smythe and her bunch," said Penelope. "There's Pinkers Rathbone. That must be about the stupidest name for a pony ever!"

Annie looked with curiosity at the pretty bay pony tied to the side of the trailer and at Anneli Smythe, who was undoing the pony's leg bandages. Already she felt out of place in her jeans when everyone else seemed to be wearing jodhpurs, and she longed for the feel of her magic riding clothes.

Tumbling from the car, Annie came face-to-face with Anneli, who smiled.

32

"Hello," she said. "Are you a friend of Penelope's?"

Before Annie could answer, Penelope interrupted. "She's my groom, that's all. Come on, Annie."

"Groom! Lucky you." Anneli turned to Annie with a questioning look. "I hope she's paying you well."

"Oh, she's not paying me at all. I'm doing it because . . ." But Annie couldn't bring herself to say — because I've never been to a horse show before. Instead she said, ". . . for fun." This surprised Anneli, who was about to say something else when an older girl, who looked a lot like her, appeared around the truck carrying a hay net.

"Hurry up, Anneli, we're deciding on our entries. You can tie this up."

Anneli made a face, then cheerfully

picked up the hay net. "Bossy older sister," she explained. "Here you are, Pinkie." She tied the hay net to the ring on the side of the truck.

"Is that the entries for the show-jumping competition?" Annie asked.

"That's right. I think I'll be doing the Junior Class. I usually do." Before Annie could ask any more questions, Penelope steamed toward them.

"Annie Deakin! You tell lies! What do you mean by leaving this in the back of the trailer? Pebbles could have caught his foot in it and had a terrible accident." Annie stared in astonishment at the backpack Penelope held out. She knew for certain she had left it on the tack room floor. Dropping it, Penelope turned on her heel in disgust.

Annie knew there was only one possible way the backpack could have gotten in the trailer. She hurried to the back ramp as Penelope led Pebbles out the front. Ned must have put it there. But there was no sign of him, big or small, and she wondered if he was hiding somewhere in the straw. She looked across the busy show ground. Ned could not be his big self here. People would think he was a loose pony and rush to catch him.

"Out of the way, Annie," said Mrs. Potter, all efficiency. "I want to put up the back ramp so we can tie Pebbles to it. You can keep an eye on him while Penelope and I sort out her jumping entry. If there's any problems, give Anneli's big sister a shout."

"Or me," said Anneli. "I can help."

"Thank you, Anneli," said Mrs. Potter. Once Pebbles was secured, she set off for the secretary's tent, followed by a sulking Penelope.

"You're braver than I am," Anneli confided. "I wouldn't be Penelope's groom for anything." And she went back to rolling bandages. Annie gave Pebbles a pat. He seemed resigned to wait and flicked an ear to rid himself of an annoying fly.

Before picking up her backpack, she stood uncertain, wanting to look for Ned. She was about to dump it in the back of the car when, from inside the trailer, she heard a low whicker. Annie hurried up the front ramp to find the big Ned standing, tacked up and ready. Over his bridle was a leather halter, and a lead rope hung neatly coiled underneath. His mane was in tidy braids. The backpack slid to the floor and Annie flung her arms around the pony's chestnut neck.

"I thought I'd missed you! But you're here."

Ned nuzzled her arm with his nose.

"Careful of my mane. I've come dressed for the occasion."

"It's show jumping," said Annie. "We can watch it together."

"Not *watch* it," said the pony. "*Do* it! I've got it all worked out."

Annie stepped back in surprise. "You mean, me and you do the show-jumping competition?"

"That's exactly what I mean. You don't think we've done all that nighttime show-jumping practice for nothing, do you? Now, ask that girl Anneli to keep an eye on Pebbles. Tell her you're going to look around the show ground."

"But . . . !"

"Go on, before Penelope and Mrs. Potter get back."

"Right," said Annie and, hurrying outside, she jumped from the ramp.

Pebbles was dozing quietly with his head in the shade, and Anneli was grooming Pinkie's tail.

"Excuse me," said Annie. The girl turned and smiled. "Could you keep an eye on Pebbles while I have a look around?"

"Sure," said Anneli. "No problem." She looked over Annie's shoulder and pointed. "They're on their way back, anyway."

"Thanks very much," said Annie, catching sight of Penelope trailing a

number card. She darted back around the trailer and quickly climbed the ramp.

"Put on your backpack and mount," said Ned. Annie pushed her arms through the straps. "And be careful not to hit your head on the roof." The moment Annie put a foot in the stirrup, they heard Penelope's strident tones outside.

"What do you mean she's gone to look around?"

"Then you'll have to get Pebbles ready by yourself," said Mrs. Potter.

"But Annie should be doing it. That's what she's here for." Slowly, oh, so slowly, Annie eased herself up, terrified she would make a bang or a clunk before she was on Ned's back. "She's got some nerve."

Crouching low, Annie slid into the saddle. The moment she was there, the familiar blast of magic wind blew and she and Ned were spun away until they were a tiny pony and a tiny rider, cantering across the rubber matting on the floor. Ahead, a black ditch — which Annie knew was the gap between the door and the ramp — needed jumping. She leaned forward, ready for takeoff. Ned leaped and, once on the other side, charged down the ramp. He took each antislip bar in his stride before his final leap onto the grass and his dash for the underneath of the car. They regained their breath while Penelope's towering riding boots brushed past on her way to collect Pebbles's saddle and bridle.

Now Annie wore magic riding clothes — a black velvet hard hat, navy blue jacket, jodhpurs, and jodhpur boots. She felt behind for her backpack, but it was gone. Across Ned's back, behind the saddle, lay a pair of saddlebags.

"Can I look inside?" she asked.

"Please do!"

Annie stretched around and undid a buckle. Inside was her sandwich box. She looked in the other bag and found her can of lemonade, bottle of water, the two apples, and banana.

"My picnic!" she cried.

"I'm glad I noticed you'd left it behind."

"Thank you, Ned." And just to check, Annie felt in the little pocket at the waistband of her jodhpurs. Yes, her change purse was tucked safely away, too.

"It's time for breakfast," she said, opening the sandwich box. "Now I've got everything I need."

"Everything except an entry number," said Ned.

Annie looked alarmed. "I'd forgotten about that. How can I get one? And what will I do if Penelope sees me?"

"She won't, because I have a plan."

"What is it?" asked Annie, wishing she could keep wearing her magic riding clothes. But the moment she dismounted and let go of the reins, they would vanish.

"Breakfast first, plan after." Ned wobbled his lips around the apple that Annie offered.

"Good idea," said Annie, who was starving. She took a large bite from a sandwich and, while they both chewed, she wondered what Ned's plan might be.

Chapter 4

Entries

"OK," said Ned, swallowing the last of his apple and peering around the black rim of car tire. "Hold tight! It's time to put my plan into action." He trotted out from under the car into a blinding wind, which spun them tall. When they walked past Pebbles, they were a normal-sized pony and rider, just like anyone else in the show ground. Penelope, busy tacking up, didn't give them a second glance.

"As always, you have the perfect disguise," whispered Ned before quickening his pace.

Annie did her best rising trot as they sped between the trailers. When they neared the white tent, Ned slowed down.

"This is where we try out the plan," he said, walking into the shade of a spreading oak tree. "At the base of my mane, near the saddle, you'll find a few loose hairs. Pull one out."

"But, Ned . . ."

"Go on."

Annie chose a chestnut hair with care and quickly pulled. Ned stamped a foot and snorted.

"Did it hurt?" she asked.

"A mere pinprick. Now wind it around your finger."

Annie wound it around the first finger of her left hand, but the hair was springy and kept trying to come loose. She held it with her thumb and stuck her fingers together to keep it in place.

"Now get off," Ned said.

Annie dismounted and let go of the

reins, expecting the riding clothes to disappear, but they didn't.

"Excellent," said the pony. "All you have to do now is tie me to the tree and you can go. But remember — if the hair falls off, the magic will vanish and so will the riding clothes. Keep the hair on your finger to keep the magic in place. That hair will only work once."

Tying Ned up and adjusting the stirrups was easier said than done with such a springy hair to hold on to, but after a lot of fumbling Annie managed it.

"Well done," said Ned. "Enter in the Junior Jumping, that's the same class as Penelope's. You'll have to pay."

Annie remembered her money. "I've got my coin purse."

"Good luck," said Ned, turning to watch her go.

The jodhpur boots were especially stiff after sneakers and Annie arrived at the white tent feeling strangely different. A sign outside said SHOW SECRETARY and, rather shyly, she joined the line in front of the secretary's table, glad there was no one there she knew.

It was quite a shock when Anneli and her sister took the place behind her. She kept her back to them, unable to help overhearing what they said.

"It looks like you and Penelope Potter are going to be in the same class again," said the older sister.

"Don't remind me. At least I don't have to be bossed around like that poor girl who came as her groom." Annie felt herself go hot and pink.

"Next," said the lady behind the desk. "Next," she said again before Annie realized it was her turn.

"I'd like to enter the Junior Show Jumping Class please."

"Name?"

"Annie . . ." She stopped. She couldn't use her real name. "Smith," she said.

"Annie Smith," repeated the lady, writing it down. "Pony's name."

"Ned." She wrote that down, too.

"Number twenty-seven." The lady pushed a number card and strings across the table. "That's two dollars and fifty cents."

Two dollars and fifty cents! Annie fumbled in her pocket for her purse. It was more than she thought, and she wasn't sure she had enough money. She put the purse in her left hand. Her thumb slipped and the magic hair started to unroll. The lady tapped her pen on her clipboard. She had a line. Annie became flustered and her face grew pinker. Managing to undo the zipper at last, she picked out first one dollar and then two.

"And fifty cents," said the lady.

Annie put down ten, twenty, forty, forty-two, forty-seven, forty-nine cents and the purse was empty. One end of the hair sprang free. Sweat dribbled down the back of Annie's neck; she had never felt so hot in her life. She shook the purse and one final, surprising penny rolled across the table. The lady scooped it up. "Next."

Annie didn't dare look around. Ned's magic hair had nearly unraveled. She shoved her coin purse in her pocket and grabbed her number. Outside, she scooted behind the white canvas walls of the tent, where the hair finally sprang into the air. Both it and the magic riding clothes vanished.

"Hey, Annie, I've been looking for you everywhere!" As quick as she could, Annie stuffed her number under her sweatshirt before turning to find Penelope storming toward her. "I've had to do everything all by myself. A fine groom you've turned out to be."

"I'm sorry. I just went to take a little look around. Anneli was keeping an eye on Pebbles. I thought you wouldn't mind."

"Oh, no, I don't mind tacking up, brushing out Pebbles's tail, and putting on the tendon boots all by myself when I'm supposed to have a groom. Well, you can just come along and finish up. I need to change."

Annie sighed and glanced to where Ned was tethered. She had no choice, so she trudged behind Penelope back to the trailer. From the shade of the oak tree, Ned watched her go. Annie didn't dare look back. It was obvious what had happened.

"Oh, there you are, Annie," said Mrs. Potter vaguely. "I wondered where you'd gone."

"I was having a look around."

Penelope flung her head back crossly. "Instead of helping me."

Annie bit her lip and looked at her shoes. Penelope had managed perfectly well without her, and all the other riders seemed to be getting their own ponies ready. But it was true she hadn't helped much.

"Well, get on with it."

As there was really nothing left to do,

Annie decided to paint on one final coat of hoof oil. The tin and brush were sitting invitingly in the grooming box. Pebbles swished his tail at the occasional fly while she got busy. By the time Penelope had changed, Annie had applied the finishing touch.

"I would have let you have a ride on Pebbles if you'd been a proper groom. Now I won't." Penelope swung herself into the saddle. "I'm going to practice. The Junior Show Jumping is going to start soon. If you watch, you might learn something." She turned Pebbles and set off in the direction of the show-jumping ring.

"Is there somewhere to practice?" Annie asked.

"Oh, yes," said Mrs. Potter. "There's a practice jump in the collecting ring. That's the place where the riders wait until it's their turn to jump. I've time for a quick cup of tea before I make my way there. Then I'll show you if you like."

"No, it's OK. I'll find it." Annie set off in the opposite direction of Penelope.

"It's the other way," called Mrs. Potter, but when Annie took no notice, she shrugged and went to dig out her thermos.

Annie hurried back to the oak tree where Ned was waiting for her.

"I lost the hair, but it's all right. Penelope's practicing in the collecting ring."

"And we must, too," Ned said.

Annie pulled out her number from underneath her sweatshirt and tied the strings around her waist so that the twenty-seven showed on her back. Next, she undid the halter and took it off. She gasped with surprise as it disappeared into thin air.

"Sorry," said Ned. "I should have warned you that we won't need the halter anymore."

Lifting off the saddlebags, she found herself holding her backpack. She leaned it against the tree and pulled down the stirrup irons. The moment her bottom touched the saddle, the magic riding clothes appeared with the number twenty-seven showing clearly on her back. She was ready at last.

Chapter 5

The Blue Ribbon

They found the collecting ring easily. It was a roped-off area next to the show-jumping arena. Spectators milled around waiting for the Junior Show Jumping to begin and inside the collecting ring Annie saw Penelope on Pebbles, in front of Anneli on Pinkie, lining up for the practice jump.

Counting the jumps in the show-jumping ring set her heart fluttering with excitement.

"There are nine, Ned. Nine huge jumps! Look at the size of that wall. It's so big, it's scary."

"We can do it," said Ned. "Let's practice. But remember, once we mingle with the others, I'll only be able to whisper."

"I'll whisper back," said Annie.

They went into the collecting ring to join the riders in line. Faces turned to look at her, and Annie tried to smile but was suddenly nervous. When it was their turn, Ned set off at such a pace that Annie was almost left behind. He took off while she was still struggling to balance, and she landed halfway up his neck. The practice jump clattered to the ground behind them and, to her horror, Annie found herself rolling forward, unable to stop. She somersaulted gently over Ned's shoulder to land with a bump and was left clinging tightly to the reins, desperate not to lose her magic riding clothes in front of everyone.

"Well held," whispered Ned.

Annie, shaking with fright, scrambled back into the saddle feeling ashamed of herself. It was only a little jump. What was it going to be like when she had the big red wall to face? Thank goodness she had managed to keep hold of the reins.

"Think what would have happened if I'd ended up on the ground in my jeans and sweatshirt," she whispered.

"Everyone would have had a big surprise," chuckled Ned. "Come on, we can do better than that."

He turned to join the line for another try, passing Penelope and Pebbles on the way. Annie didn't miss the familiar sneer.

"Lucky Penelope doesn't know it's me."

"It's just nerves. You'll soon get over them," was Ned's whispered reply.

Annie hoped so. The last thing she wanted was for her and Ned to send all the competition jumps crashing to the ground. She watched Penelope and Pebbles clear the practice jump with ease and winced at Penelope's superior *that's how to do it* look as she cantered past. Annie took a deep breath. It was her fault Ned had knocked the jump down last time. This time they must clear it.

For their second try, Annie was better prepared and they flew over.

"When we take off together, it's so easy." She laughed as they cantered around in a circle. "Let's hope we can do it like this in the show-jumping ring."

"We will," Ned assured her. "We will."

"Any more competitors for the Junior Jumping whose numbers aren't on the board?" a lady called.

Annie rode over to the blackboard standing by the entrance to the show-jumping arena.

"I haven't put my number down," she told the lady. "It's twenty-seven."

The lady chalked up twenty-seven at the bottom of the list.

"Looks like you're going last, dear," she said as the loudspeaker crackled and an announcement began.

"The Junior Show Jumping is about to begin and the first competitor to go is number eleven, Justin Spencer, riding Bongo."

A tingling sensation ran up Annie's spine and she rode Ned to the edge of the collecting ring to watch. This was it.

The moment she had always longed for. Unexpectedly, Penelope's voice boomed behind her.

"Anneli, my groom's disappeared again. You haven't seen her, have you? She's been absolutely useless. And did you see that girl on the chestnut pony fall off? How hopeless can you get?"

"How rude," said Ned, under his breath. Annie grew pink with embarrassment and pretended not to hear.

"Penelope, everyone falls off," said Anneli. "It's part of learning how to ride better."

"I don't."

"We'll just have to wait and see about that, won't we?" said Anneli. Penelope rode off in a huff.

Sometimes Penelope can be really

mean, thought Annie. Still, it made her determined to do her best. She concentrated on the boy and his pony racing around the course. Bongo took out a brick at the wall and then splashed into the water. Justin Spencer collected a disappointing eight faults. He was not to be the only one. Competitor after competitor left the ring with fallen jumps behind them. Even Anneli and Pinkie knocked two bricks from the wall. Nobody seemed able to manage a clear round.

"We'll watch Penelope and then have another practice jump to put us in the mood," said Ned when it was Penelope's turn.

Pebbles trotted into the arena and Penelope urged him into a canter. With his silver tail flowing, he cleared jump after jump until he came to the wide water. Maybe it was the shadow of a bird or maybe the water was a surprise, but whatever it was, at the last moment Pebbles stopped and skidded into the poles. He sent Penelope spiraling over his head to land with a mighty splash. By the time she stood up, she was soaked.

"Mmm," whispered Ned. "What was it Penelope said about never falling off?"

"Oh, dear," said Annie. "That's going to put her in a really bad mood."

They turned for the practice jump and Annie soon forgot about Penelope as she and Ned soared over the single pole, not once but twice. Then, before she was expecting it, her name was called over the loudspeaker.

"And the last to go in the Junior Show Jumping is number twenty-seven, Annie Smith, riding Ned."

"It's us!" She gasped. "And it's scary."

"It doesn't have to be," said Ned. "So far, there are no clear rounds. All we need to do is jump without knocking anything down and we've won."

"Do you think we can do it?"

"We'll give it a try," he whispered and trotted into the arena.

They cantered in an elegant circle waiting for the start bell to ring. Annie sat up, trying to look her best, feeling the gaze of the crowd on her. Then the bell sounded and she glued her eyes to the first jump, an inviting rustic cross pole.

Cantering toward it, Annie felt a flutter in her tummy, yet the moment they cleared it her nerves vanished. The bigger blue-and-white upright was next but Annie was ready for it and, even while they were in the air, they began the turn that would take them to the fir-tree hedge.

Now Annie had the attention of the crowd. Ponies and riders gathered to watch this unknown girl on her chestnut pony, but Annie was too busy to notice. Having cleared the fir-tree hedge, she and Ned had the problem of the tricky double.

"It'll be jump stride jump," panted Ned. "Hang on tight."

Ned's feet pounded the grass and the first part of the double was upon them. He leaped into the air. Annie leaned

forward for the stride in the middle and they were in the air again, clearing it without mishap. Ned was going at such speed, there was hardly time to think as they turned across the arena for the parallel. Beyond its yellow-and-white poles loomed the giant red wall.

"Steady, steady, Ned," Annie said as they soared over the parallel and cantered purposefully to the big red wall. Annie was alarmed by the size of it, but

there was no stopping now as Ned reared up against the large rectangular bricks. There was a gasp from the crowd but, to Annie's relief, they landed safely on the other side without a brick out of place.

Next was the race to the water jump. The wind whistled as Ned galloped flat out. He took off with a long stretching jump, determined not to put a foot in the water. They landed clear.

"Slow down, Ned, slow," said Annie, realizing they had to slow down if they were going to get safely over the staircase, which was coming up fast.

Ned had trouble steadying himself and they took off at a funny angle. This unbalanced Annie and caused Ned to rap the top pole with his hind leg. Had it fallen? Gathering up the reins, Annie didn't dare look back until they had cleared the painted barrels and raced through the finish line. She could hardly believe it — the pole was still in place! From around the show ring, the spectators applauded the only clear round. Annie and Ned had won.

It was Annie's best daydream come true when she and Ned were presented with the first-prize blue ribbon. She clipped it proudly to Ned's bridle and led the way in the lap of honor, cantering out of the show-jumping arena with applause still ringing in her ears.

Arriving back at the oak tree, Annie's face wore the widest of smiles. She

dismounted, unpinned the blue ribbon, and flung her arms around Ned's neck.

"Thank you for everything," she said.

Ned gave her an affectionate nuzzle with his nose. "You can take me back to the trailer in your backpack," he said. "I could do with a rest."

Annie let go of the reins and her magic riding clothes vanished. So did Ned. Back in her ordinary clothes, she opened the backpack. The tiny Ned cantered from behind the oak tree and jumped inside. Annie carefully placed the blue ribbon beside him. Knowing Penelope must never see it, she did up the straps. The number twenty-seven she threw in the trash can on her way back to the trailer to help.

Penelope's expression was grim.

"I suppose everyone knows I fell off. Just don't mention it, that's all," she warned.

"I won't," said Annie. "I'm really sorry you did."

"I'd like to tell that girl who won a thing or two. Now she thinks she's the best. But she fell off in the collecting ring. If you ask me, her winning was the most amazing fluke."

Anneli, who was putting a tail bandage on Pinkie, shook her head. "Nonsense, Penelope, she won because she rode well. That's all there is to it."

"You keep out of it, Anneli Smythe.

Just mind your own business." Annie
hated it when Penelope was so rude. She
gave Anneli an apologetic smile and
carefully put her backpack in the car.

Driving home was a silent affair. Annie secretly let Ned out to stretch his legs and laid the remaining apple on the floor for him to chew. Trying not to spill any crumbs, she ate the last of her sandwiches. More than anything, she wanted to get home and pin the blue ribbon next to Ned's poster on the wall.

It was almost four o'clock when she left Ned jumping up the fig-tree leaves to her bedroom before hurrying around to the back door to let herself in.

"Did you have a good time?" Mom asked.

"Awesome," said Annie, noticing a delicious-looking cherry cake sitting ready on a plate. "There's just one thing I've got to do, and then I'll tell you all about it."

"Did Penelope win?"

"No, it was a girl called Annie Smith riding a pony called Ned."

"Isn't Ned the name of the pony in your poster?"

"Yes. Isn't that funny?" said Annie and hurried upstairs.

In her bedroom, she found Ned back in his picture and quickly pinned the blue ribbon next to him.

"Thank you, Ned, it was a day to remember forever and ever."

"Who are you talking to?"

Annie swung around to find Jamie standing in the doorway with his magician's cloak draped over his shoulders and his magic wand in his hand. "And where did you get that ribbon?"

"From the horse show."

"Didn't win it, did you?"

"I might have."

"Pull the other leg, Annie. That's an old one of Penelope's, I bet."

"A good guess," said Annie, not saying whether it was or wasn't and, before Jamie had time to ask any more awkward questions, she hurried downstairs.

It was a relief when she could sink into

an armchair and bite into a large piece of
cherry cake. She chewed slowly, relishing
the taste, thinking of Ned. To have a
magic pony was the best thing ever! She
glowed with happiness, smiled a secret
smile, and took another bite.